I0738525

Three X's the Dream

RAYVEN MANIGO

Three X's the Dream

By Rayven Manigo

Cover Created by Jazzy Kitty Publications

Logos by Andre M. Saunders/Jess Zimmerman

Editor: Anelda L. Attaway

Co-Editor: Rayven Manigo

© 2020 Rayven Manigo

ISBN 978-1-7349014-6-7

Library of Congress Control Number: 2020913897

DEDICATION

To every writer, your dreams can be fulfilled with God, prayer and commitment. Stay focused, believe, and achieve, someone is waiting for your gift!!

ACKNOWLEDGMENTS

Philippians 4:13 NIV: I can do all this through him who gives me strength.

What an amazing journey this has been. This seemed surreal, not knowing if my friends and family were just telling me "wow, this is great" to spare my feelings, or if it was in fact really great. Only time will tell!!! There were times giving up, saying I'm done, making excuse after excuse took total damnation over my life. But how many people know God will send someone to encourage you? He will send someone to help you see YOU GOT THIS!! Your faith may be tested, but your testimony will be great!!

TABLE OF CONTENTS

INTRODUCTION

Challenges are often depicted as a contest or competition. This describes the vibe for these short stories.

A real challenge, a competition I had within. Wanting to venture out and try a different approach, without ridicule or judgment, if you ever want something bad enough, you'll get it, regardless of you being your own critic!!

Within this book, you'll dive into three different stories. Each story has unique flare and character, real life, real events, their truths unveiled. I hope you enjoy.

STORY I

The Accident

Her elegant daze was halted by an embrace to her frontal lobe, "Hey Baby."

There stood a tall, chocolate specimen of a man. . . he must be mistaken.

"Wait, do I know him? Why's he here? Why am I here?" Levi said to herself.

Levi was confused, ever since the accident she struggled to remember her own name. Troy sat close to her with pictures in what appeared to be a wedding album, an ivory dress neatly draped upon her shoulders, a bushel of sunflowers mixed with red roses graced her hands and he was standing beside her showing all his pearly white teeth.

"Ugh, why can't I remember?? Why????! Troy, is that right? This doesn't make sense."

"I woke up, you were beside my bed in what I'm told was a miraculous recovery. 21 days in a coma, only to be able to walk, talk, and move my limbs.

"But Ummm," she said as she closed her eyes and clinched her fist, "damn!! Why is this so hard?!!!"

Let's rewind, rain droplets hit the surface of her car as she glided out the parking lot in her anniversary present, a 2020 G-Wagon.

She reached over pressing the call button, "Hey Troy, what you want for dinner tonight?"

"Hmmm. . . besides you?" He had a distinct tone when talking to Levi, what some women dreamt of.

"Boyyy stop it, I've been working hard all day, all I want is to make a good dinner, eat, catch up on 'Tiger King' and go to bed."

"Girl, you didn't say anything about love on your man?"

"Oh, I didn't plan on it. . ." BAM!!!!

"Levi!!! Levi!!! Levi!!! What's wrong?!!! Baby talk to me!! What's happening? Levi. . ."

The phone silenced as Levi's car hung onto an embankment. An unconscious Levi, clinging to her death; unbeknownst to her this is where the confusion begun.

Over 21 days later. . .

Dr. Randolph reported, "Levi, you hit your head on the steering wheel, now you have what appears to be retrograde amnesia. This can affect your memory short-term, or long-term." Tears exited her face.

He continued, "Troy the best thing for you to do is take her home and familiarize her with memories."

Troy and Levi were newlyweds, he was already upholding those vows, *"through sickness and health"* but he knew Levi would do the same for him.

"Are you ready?"

"Ready as I'll ever be," she said those words with a trembling voice.

Troy paraded her through their hometown Biloxi, Mississippi.

"Baby see, this is where we met. . . You were

coming out of the courthouse dressed in the most beautiful two-piece suit, every inch of material hit just right. And I was entering, paying off a traffic ticket. I purposely bumped into you; you smacked your teeth and with the most disturbed look piercing my soul. I knew then, I had to have you!!!"

"Wow, so I gave you my number, just like that?"

"No, you made me work for it. Every day for five days straight I got off work, I came to the courthouse and bumped into you. Until finally. . ."

"What did I do, call the police?"

"Naw, Baby you said, 'at least buy me a cup of coffee' and the rest was history!!!"

With a smirk, she whispered, "What happened next?!"

Troy continued telling stories, attempting to spark her memory. Until Levi saw a man coming from the bank,

"Ummm. . . Troy, I know him." Unbeknownst to Levi, Troy knew him too.

"Isn't he. . . wait. . . is that a man I've dated? Could he be my husband?"

Levi exclaimed, "No!!!" shouted Troy, "I am!!!"

"Well, I remembered something," Levi closed her eyes and began, "it was a cold night, my tire blew out, and this man came to my rescue; he had a dark complexion with a tattoo on his arm that read "Philippians 4:13." I remember because that's one of my favorite scriptures. We exchanged numbers, I met him for coffee, and we got married!!! Why am I here with you? Troy, who are you?"

"I'm your husband."

"Then who is he? What's happening?" Troy silenced Levi with his index finger close to her lips.

"Baby, I'm here, I'll take care of you."

"But. . ."

"Shhh!! Let me handle everything."

Levi tossed and turned in the spare bedroom of a three-bedroom, two-story modern home within a gated community. She still didn't understand how she thought she recognized the man at the bank but didn't know the man who claimed to be her husband.

She thought to herself, *"If only I knew who my family was maybe they could make the connection. Troy said both of my parents died a couple of years ago and I'm the only child. Damn, my life sucks!!"* Tap, Tap!!

"Levi Baby, are you up?"

Tap, Tap, Tap, Tap, "Levi. . ."

A silence fell over the room as Levi didn't want Troy to know she was awake. In deep thought she contemplated running away or climbing out the window. However, since her size 12 jeans were barely buttoning, she was unsure of the outcome and the trajectory of the fall. Therefore, she closed her eyes and held her breath; surely he'd go away.

"Nooo, move away, leave me alone! Why?! What's happening? Where am I?"

"Levi!! Levi!! You're having a dream, wake up,

wake up!!" Levi was awoken to sweat gleaming on her forehead and her bed cover on the floor.

"What's wrong, what happened in your dream?" Troy exclaimed.

"I'm okay."

However, Levi wasn't okay her memory was slowly returning.

Months had passed since leaving the hospital. Levi was finally able to remember a few things from her past. However, some things were still unclear. Troy kept a pretty close proximity at all times. And within this gated community houses were spread apart, it's like an epidemic, shelter in place was an everyday occurrence.

"What am I to do? I can't ask Troy because I know he's not telling me something."

Levi devised a plan, *"When he's sound asleep, I'm going to take my chances, jump from the window and pray I land directly on that rose bush. Roses!!!*

Roses, they were in my wedding. But, Troy told me he was allergic to roses. Who is he really?"
Thump!! Bam!

"Ouch!!! I hope I can walk after this."

Levi stood up with a slight pause to catch her breath, it's not every day you jump from a second story window unto roses.

"Now where do I go?"

It was 2:00 a.m., Troy was sound asleep. And Levi on the hunt for her identity. Levi followed the paved driveway to a road and she turned left; hoping for the best!! She ducked behind a pecan tree when headlights approached; she wasn't taking any chances. She had to figure out who she really was!! She walked what felt like 15 miles, the time read 3:43. There's only a few places open this late, Whataburger, the hospital, and the police station. If only she can get to the police station.

"Woohh!! Ohhh! Ugh!! I'm tired!! I'm sure Troy

is looking for me everywhere it's now 5:30, time for his morning run. I need to run too if I want to run into my actual life!"

Levi stayed the course and landed at a police station. She discussed with the officer the events.

"Sir, I think I was kidnapped. I know my name is Levi. Well, I think? I'm married to someone named Troy. We live in a gated community several miles from town! I walked here because something isn't right!!"

Officer Johnson reported, "Ma'am, you look so familiar. Are you sure you live in a gated community several miles from town?!?!"

"Listen! All I know, I hit my head, the doctor said I can't remember and I'm about tired of this crazy shit!!!"

"Yes Ma'am, hold on I'll be right back!!"

She immediately said to herself, *"What does he know? Is my name really Levi? Sweet Jesus from on high, the Lily of the Valley, the Bright and Morning*

Star!! I know, I absolutely know I haven't been staying with a man that ain't my husband!!"

Officer Johnson returned, "Ma'am, is this you?"

Tears formed in Levi's eyes, her name was actually Levingston and she's married to a lawyer named Troy!! She works for a courthouse and he became a lawyer for the same courthouse.

"Ma'am, people have been looking for you for several months. The day of the accident, your husband Troy was asked to leave, something about a virus running crazy in the streets and claiming many African American lives. He left you there for recovery. So many doctors and nurses were changed because of falling victim to this illness. The President reports this being a pandemic, all I know is we can't leave the house. However, you know our people are still going Facebook live with more than 10 people, having "virus" parties and making TikTok videos. But. . . Enough of that. . . This man, you said his name was Troy. And he picked you up from the hospital?"

Levi, spoke in a muffled tone, "Dr. Randolph told Troy to take me home to familiarize myself with memories. He took me down several streets and pointed out places he said we went together. But then, a man came out of a bank, he looked so familiar, I thought I was married to him."

"Did he look like this?"

"Yessss!!!! That's him. Who is he?"

"Levi that's your husband, he's the real Troy!!!"

Dazed and confused, Levi slouched her shoulders and screamed out, "What's going on?! Officer Johnson you have to help me, my memory is coming back but evidently it's not fully here. I know I'm married; I know what the doctor said, and I know where I've been living for several months. But, I don't even know how we got here."

Levi a bit shaken tried to piece together her life leading to this point with the help of Officer Johnson.

She mentioned, "Maybe we should start at the hospital there has to be guidance there."

"But wait, shouldn't we call the real Troy?"

"And by the way what's my last name? Do I have family here? Am I really the only child? Do I have kids? Dogs? I'm sure I wouldn't have cats or do I?"

Officer Johnson smirked with the internal questioning. He didn't know the answer to majority of those questions. What he did know was where to find Troy; the real Troy!! Backing out of the police station a white van appeared with the words, *"We Can Beat Any Quote."*

Levi shouted, "That's the fake Troy's van, that's him, that's him!"

Levi remembered those words on a business card as well, but she wasn't entirely sure. Officer Johnson wrote down the license plate, but he didn't apprehend as to not draw attention to Levi. The pair drove down a familiar street.

"This is where he took me, he said we met right

there. The bank is across the street where I saw the other man who I knew I was married to. Yes!!! Memory!!! Yesssss!!!"

Officer Johnson parked while Troy waited in the car. Inside the building, he stopped at a receptionists desk.

"Hello, I'm here with information concerning Troy's wife, is he in?"

"Yes, he's here. One second. . ." Stacey called back to his office with a less than enthusiastic voice, "Troy an officer is here to speak with you concerning Levi!" A scream came from around the corner, "Please God let her be alright!!!" Officer Johnson entered the office.

"Troy, I have great news."

Stacey interjected, "Do y'all need anything?"

"No, please exit and close the door!! Hold all of my calls!!! Officer Johnson please continue."

"Levi is in my car, she's retaining some memory, however, she's been held captive by a man pretending to be you."

Shocked and confused Troy uttered, "What??"

Stacey thought to herself, *"Gosh!! What is taking so long, I'm ready to meet the real Troy!!! The white van circled the parking lot three times since they've been in there and I'm hoping he doesn't see me in here. Maybe I should crawl back to the trunk?!?! Nah, I'll be okay, I wish he would hurry."* Inside the office, Stacey made a phone call.

"Terry!!! Did you not handle our little problem? What did I pay you for? She survived the accident, you kidnapped her from the hospital, but somehow you managed to let her escape?!?! And what makes matters worse, Troy is happy again!!! I'm supposed to be Mrs. Gates. Ugh, you don't do nothing right!!!! Where is she now Terry? Bye!! Here they come!!!"

"Hey Mr. Gates, Levi was found. That's great news!!!! Where is she? Is she okay? Does she remember anything?"

Stacey was very eager to get information on Levi;

little did they know she orchestrated the entire thing. Picture it, Stacey and Terry are brother and sister.

Stacey handles all of Mr. Gates financial obligations as well as answers the phone, makes him coffee, and pretends to care about his troubles. Stacey devised a plan to seduce Mr. Gates, win over his heart, and eventually his last name. But, there's a problem with that, Mrs. Gates is head over heels for her husband and he loves her just as hard!! He's not a cheater. Yea she's got a good one. So Stacey decides to get her brother involved. The Gates were looking for an interior designer and someone to renovate empty space in their home. Stacey told them about her brother and the couple decided to utilize *"We Beat Any Quote"* something they'd soon regret.

Walking to the car, Troy's knees buckled a few times. It's been 156 days since he's seen Levi and the anticipation was more than he could handle!! Levi opened the door and glanced at a chocolate man standing about 6'4 with a three piece suit, two of the buttons on his shirt were unbuttoned showing off smooth chocolate skin.

She bit her bottom lip thinking, *"God did You send him just for me?"*

She shook her head as to erase her current thinking, "You!! You are my husband right?!? Please say you're my husband?"

Troy stated with tears rolling down his face, "Yes, I am your husband, Mrs. Gates."

"Mrs. Gates, I'm Mrs. Gates. As in Bill Gates?!?!"

"No, close but not quite. As in Lead Executive Congresswoman Levingston Gates!!"

"Now wait one damn minute!!! I'm a congresswoman!! Like, I got an important job with important people, I carry a briefcase?!?! Like that?!!!"

Troy stated, "Yes, you see that office? I work upstairs as a lawyer in the courthouse. You, my amazing, beautiful, smart, God fearing woman are the HWIC."

"The What?"

"Head Woman in Charge!!!"

"Ooohhh!!! Say less!!!! I run shit!!!!"

"Yes, Baby you do!!!"

"Wow!!! Okay, so we're married. I run this office and my last name is Gates. I'm married to the finest man in Biloxi. I see why I was kidnapped!!! Now, speaking of being kidnapped!! What happens next?"

Troy stated, "I take my wife home!!"

With excitement in her voice, Levi stated, "I can't wait to see it!!!"

A sense of peace came over Levi!! Finally, she was safe and secure with a man she barely knew. But for some reason, that was enough!! Well, shouldn't it be?

"Wow!! This gated community is different than the other one!!! This one has a greeter, a code to

enter, it wasn't far from town. It even has a brand new G-Wagon with a hot pink bow and a license plate that read 4UX's2 sitting in someone's driveway. I am not sure who's car that is but damn!!"

Troy pulled into that very driveway, pushed a garage door button, and parked.

"Hey, Troy, I know we are just getting to know each other again. But whose vehicle is that?"

"Oh!! After the accident, yours was totaled and I didn't want to chauffeur you around town so I got you another one."

"Oh we got it like that?"

"Baby you don't know the half!!!"

Eager to know her half, his half, and everyone's half. They entered their home. Pictures of their wedding plastered on the walls. A mural of them occupied a room. She knew this was it!! A business card sat on the kitchen counter, she glanced at it. *"We Beat Any Quote."*

"TROY!!!!!!!!!! This is the man that kidnapped me!! This is him. Call Officer Johnson!!! I remember now. Hurry before I forget!!!"

"Okay, start at the beginning."

"We hired this man to do our house, I didn't have many interactions with him because I was too busy campaigning!! The day of my accident, I saw the white van in the parking lot. It left when I left, and then there was an accident!!! I left the hospital with someone who I now know is this man!! It's him!! I know it's him!!!"

"But wait, Stacey gave us his information, wasn't he her brother???"

Baby!! Baby!! Stacey's brother kidnapped me!! But why?!?!"

"Ugh!! I have to get out of here. It's only a matter of time before they come!! Hurry up Terry it's time to go!!!"

Terry and Stacey packed bags, with attempts to

skip town. Unbeknownst to them, Officer Johnson's eager demeanor would catch them dead in their tracks!!

"Stacey, Terry we have the house surrounded! Come out with your hands up or we will be forced to enter!"

Stacey yelled, "Wait a minute, this is not how this should go, I'm supposed to be Mrs. Gates."

"Terry!!! Terry!!! This is all your fault!! If you would have just hit the car harder or at a different angle or hell even just killed Levi we wouldn't be here!! What's wrong with you? Why can't you do anything right?!?!"

Across town, Levi and Troy were gazing at the T.V. The live recording of the standoff is making global news!!

"Well Troy, if she wanted to be famous, she's surely getting her wish!!"

Troy numb to all that's happening, trying to wrap his mind around the past several months. Glancing at

Levi with admiration, thankfulness, and gratitude he whispered, "I'm so grateful you're back!!"

Troy was thankful that Levi's amnesia overtook the trauma she should be experiencing. She's forgotten so much that she's unable to really feel all the affects it had on her. But it's my commitment to our vows, I'll take care of her through sickness and health!!

Peeping through the blinds, from what appeared to be an eternity. Stacey pondered suicide and even contemplated homicide.

"I mean it is Terry's fault!! All I wanted was a big house on a hill, a few kids, a nanny, and maybe even a pool. But here we are peeping through blinds trying to decide whether to run or end it all!! Time was ticking!! Taking the phrase WE AIN'T COMING OUT, literally!! But I would hate to know what happens if they came in. The seconds hand on the clock was ticking so loud, I thought I would just

die!!

"Come out with your hands up, Stacey and Terry!! We know you're in there!! Come out now, we can work all this out!"

Terry rushed through the door leaving Stacey without warning. He saw it on her face, she didn't care who she hurt as long as it wasn't her.

Officer Johnson handcuffed Terry, read him his rights, and placed him in the patrol car.

Stacey not sure of what to do, faced a terrible thought, *"I'm too pretty to go to prison, they will have a field day with me. Three hots and a cot, or thug it out with the Devil."* Bang!!!

Stacey committed the unthinkable act. One fatal shot ended it all!! One fatal shot took her life!! And that shot was all it took for Terry to have an alibi!!

The End!!!

STORY II

Boaz is That You?

"Girl, did you see Tyrone fine ass last night?!! Now wait. . . before you answer that, yes, everyone knows he's married. But, with just a little time with me, he may be singing a different tune. Trish did you hear me?!"

"Yes, Shellie. Every time you tell one of your scandalous stories I have to wash my mind out with soap!!"

"Your mind?"

"Yes, my mind!!! You trying to send me straight to Hell as an accomplice?!?!"

"All I'm saying is, Tyrone makes me want to "Leave the one I'm with and start a new relationship with him."

"Alright Shellie, quote another Usher song if you want to. But don't leave out "Let it burn" because that's exactly what will happen if you mess with Tyrone!"

"Girl, you and everyone in this town know he's the biggest hoe that walked the streets of Savannah!! They call it community. . . you know the rest!!"

"However, yes, unfortunately I did see him. With that one gold tooth shinning in the front row. He could've at least got an open face!! Ain't that what they are called?!!"

"But that's what you like, you've always enjoyed a man that's been around the block a time or two!!"

"Okay, I got it!! He's my type!! Not yours!! I'll just think of him tonight!"

"Ugh! Bye Shellie with your crazy self, I'll see you at church in the morning right?"

"Right??? Yes, I'll be there confessing all my sins that I did this week and probably get started on asking for forgiveness for next week."

"Next week?!?! Shellie, I'm not God, but I don't think it works like that. To each their own though! I ain't mad at you, "God knows your heart" That's what people at the church say. Anyway, don't be late, you know that's your motive, every Sunday! But let the doors of Club 68 open, you're beating the bouncer and the owner!!"

"Alright enough, I said I'll see you in the morning. You always acting like someone's mama! That's probably why you don't have a man now!!"

"That's fine, but what's your excuse?!?!"

"Bye!!"

"Bye!!!"

Dong Dong!! The church bell is heard buzzing while Shellie looks for a parking spot!

"Yes, I'm late again and Trish probably didn't save a seat! One day Lord! One day I'll make it to Your house on time!!"

Pastor Alonzo was heard speaking on a familiar subject "This too shall pass."

"Dang, I missed everything. . . the devotion, hymnals, and even announcements! I got to do better! If it wasn't for Saints and Sinners I would've been here!!! I mean how much scandal can one show

have? Jesus!! Now You know I try my hardest to live Holy, but why did You make sin so easy to get in?!?! My bad Jesus you're right, I'm already late. . . I'll holla at You later!"

Shellie squeezed by members on the row to a vacant spot next to Trish. The members are all used to her shenanigans, she does it every Sunday. At this point, Trish should learn to sit at the opposite end of the pew so Shellie can slide right in.

"Ugh, I wish they would move, they know I need a word from the Lord! Goodness!!" Letting out a gasp. . . *"Finally!!"* With a less than eager smirk, no eye contact needed, Trish glanced.

"It's about time you showed up, I figured one of those reality shows had you entertained. Or did you call Tyrone?!?!"

"Shhhh!!!! I mean she's already late, now y'all are talking!! Too bad Go Tell it on the Mountain Missionary Baptist Church doesn't have a balcony, because that's exactly where y'all would be!!!"

Pastor Alonzo was nearing the end of the message, he'd jumped on the pews (followed by the deacons who would pass for bouncers at Club 68) laid hands on a few missionaries, and now the rhythm to his voice began to change. Which means closing!!

"Let the church say Amen and Amen again, truly God was in this place today. Take us home choir." (Music playing) *"Reach out and touch somebody's hand, make this world a better place while you can!!"*

Pastor Alonzo began reciting. . . "Now unto Him that is able to keep you from falling, and to present you faultless before the presence of His glory with exceeding joy, to the only wise God our Savior, be glory and majesty, dominion and power, both now and forever. Amen."

"So, what's for lunch?"

"I picked last week Trish, so you pick this week."

"Hmmm. . . what do you have a taste for?"

"I don't even know! Something good, maybe with some options."

"Okay Chinese or American?"

"Let's do Chinese."

"You think it's safe? I mean the coronavirus did start there."

"Girl it's been a year, I think it's safe now!! And we are not in China!!"

Trish and Shellie agreed, "Meet ya there!!"

"Sis. Shellie, Sis Shellie. . ."

"I know that's not Pastor Alonzo."

"Yes, hello Pastor! What a mighty word today!!"

"Sis Shellie, I think if you start your morning earlier with God on your mind, you will arrive to church on time."

"You know what Pastor; you may be right because I start my morning with Saints and Sinners and a coffee with a side of Facebook. And well, you know the rest."

"Okay Sis, well, I'll be praying for you. Next week

is your week! You got this!"

"Alright, see you next week if the Lord says the same!!"

Pastor Alonzo was smitten on Shellie, but she was not First Lady material. I mean she arrived late, doesn't bother to show up for midweek service, and her name is non-existent on a tithe and offering envelope! But she's beautiful, has a beautiful smile, beautiful build.

Pastor Alonzo thought, *"She's really someone I should get to know."*

"Shellie, what did Pastor A want?"

"To tell me I need to be a better Christian."

"Shellie, I'm sure he didn't say it like that."

"Well not exactly, but I was caught off guard. His smile had me at Hello!! And I didn't want him to say goodbye. Is it bad of me to think about being a First Lady! I mean his wife passed away a few years ago. They didn't have children. He is a Pastor, so I'm sure he can get me through those pearly white gates. I mean shouldn't I at least see what could happen?"

"Shellie, I mean no disrespect when I say this. You are not First Lady material. I mean when was the last time you actually greeted your neighbor in the church. Oh that's right!! My bad!! You miss the reach out and touch part of service every Sunday! Listen, I'm your friend."

"Yes, the petty friend."

"I love you as a sister! But Pastor Alonzo wants someone who actually knows the Lord and not someone who hears about Him from Saints and Sinners!! I mean Damn Shellie, you ain't even trying to get to Heaven!!"

"Trish, yes I am, but if I'm First Lady I think that gives me a greater chance! I ain't trying to be in Hell, I heard it's hot and you know I don't like to sweat. Anyway, thank you for lunch. I will see you later!!"

Shellie stood 5'9, 215 lbs., built like a stallion!!

She had hazel colored eyes, a slender face, a slender waist, and her hips were the shape of an hourglass! A definite extrovert! Oh, and a Leo!!! But her attitude that's a different story. She's been employed to a couple of major companies because she has the brains of Einstein! However, she knows it! Trish 5'4, 165 lbs., a nice physique, braces, glasses, shy, an introverted Pisces! Meeting one night at a college party, the two hit it off. For some reason, they dressed up for Halloween in costumes, but nobody else did! They immediately stuck out! It was their freshman year, they wanted to meet people and make friends. Living in different dorms they didn't immediately cross paths. But, now they would be stuck together forever!!

Ring Ring!!! *"THINK IT'S BEST I PUT MY HEART ON ICE, HEART ON ICE, CAUSE I CAN'T BREATHE."*

"Shellie, see that's another reason you can't be First Lady. I don't think Pastor listens to Rod Wave!

Jesus help!!"

"My bad Trish, what's up?"

"I don't know if I should wear my red dress or yellow dress tomorrow for the award ceremony? What do you think? I know I look better in brighter colors because of my African skin! But it's something about that red dress!!"

"Trish, you've been at your company 15 years, they are awarding you with a 15 year pin. In a position where they said women were inadequate, make them lose consciousness!!"

"Okay, yellow it is!!"

"Bye girl, see you at the ceremony!"

"I wouldn't miss it for the world!!" (Click)

Shellie began thinking, maybe I should change my playlist, Trish may be right. If I want to change, I need to start listening to gospel. . . Cody Carnes "Run to the Father" yea that's a good one!! Because at this point, to be First Lady! I need to sprint to God!!!

"Where is Shellie? She's going to miss my pinning and she knows I don't have anyone else in my cheering section?? After being socially distanced for so long, we are still required to only have two guests. I gave my extra ticket to a friend because I only needed one. God send me a family; an already made family would be nice because I don't want to have children. I need a partner who believes the same, I mean we have to be equally yoked right?!?!"

"Finally!! I don't understand. Shellie, I told you 6:00. Why is it 6:30 and you are waltzing in here like you are auditioning for Dancing with the Stars?!?!"

"Okay, let me explain! I was praying?!?!"

"Huh?!?!"

"Yes, I was praying! On all fours, snot running everywhere. Girl, I only heard about it but I actually experienced God before I came."

"Shellie, are you for real? Did He speak to you?!?!"

"Yes, I reminded Him who I was?! But after that,

yep!!

"Okay, well let's talk after they pin me!!"

"You look like a snack today Trish! One of these men got to be interested in you. I'll watch their reaction when you walk across the platform. I'll let you know which one!!"

"Okay Girl!!"

"SHATRICIA DENISE ALEXANDER!"

"Yesss, that's my friend!!! Yess Girl!! 15 years, and y'all said she couldn't do it!!! Yess Baby!!"

Stares were felt from every person in the audience. Their faces said, this isn't a graduation, just simply a pinning! Shellie didn't care, she was a bit loud at times, center of attention but she had a kind heart, and when it came to Trish she would do whatever it takes to make sure she's happy!

Let's back up some, freshman year second semester, Trish received a phone call that would rock her world forever!

"Yes, this is Trish Alexander, who am I speaking

with?"

"Trish this is Officer Phase, there's been an accident?"

"What do you mean Officer?" Tears began to fall from her eyes, "what happened?"

"Your mom and dad were on their way to surprise you with a new car; they were following one another. Your mom veered off the road too late to miss a stalled car hitting a tree, she died on impact.

Your father didn't see the car stalling, hit it from behind pinning him in the vehicle, using the jaws of life, he was removed from the car, but died in route to the hospital.

"Nooooo!!!!" Screams piercing the room

Trish's whole world turned upside down! She was the only child; her parents were both only children. She didn't have any grandparents. The only person in her life was Shellie. The person she trusted, confided in, and told her secrets to. Her bestie, ace, friend for life!! From that moment on,

Shellie and Trish were inseparable. You didn't see one without the other. Until, they selected different majors. Trish an engineer, Shellie an accountant! But what they had in common was being Black women succeeding in life and living without regret. So, when will they find their Boaz?

"Thank you Shellie, I knew I could count on you to cheer me on, so did anyone stare at me?"

"Well, what do you think about Alex? Every time I come to your office, or call. He's always smitten with you. He shows you the most respect, I'm rooting for him. Oh and he stared the whole time you walked the platform."

See, Trish really did like Alex, but for some reason he never said anything; he was a nerd, clumsy, and goofy. He reminded her of Steve Urkel, but that was definitely her type. Trish and Shellie had very different taste, Trish was into more nerdy, educated, and the more wholesome type. Shellie, interested in more rough, maybe a felony or two type men.

"Ha! Ha! They say opposites really attract. Wait! Before I forget, tell me about your prayer Girl and you said God remembered you?! So that's even better!"

"Yes, it all happened while in the shower. Thinking about the future, actually including Pastor Alonzo and tears began to form. Have you ever just thought, God what is Your purpose for my life? I just want to live right and do right? That's what I felt. God speaking saying, it's time for me to get it together. Turning the water off, dried off, and just fell to my knees. All I could get out was "Use Me Lord!"

"Wow!! Shellie, this is only the beginning!!"

"Hey Trish, what are you doing this week leading up to Christmas?!"

"Umm, the same thing we normally do, visit your family at some point, eat, play a few games, and come home. Always last minute shopping for myself."

"Why?"

"Well, this year I was thinking we could feed the hungry and maybe participate in the Toys for Tots. I'm sure they have something like that with the church. What do you think? Maybe you can even invite

"Alex!! Shellie, I think. . . You know what?!! Never mind, yes I'm in. I'll see about inviting Alex, I don't want to look thirsty!! However, let's get more information Sunday and we will go from there. Saturday, are we still going to Club 68, Shellie? I mean, I know you want to run into Tyrone."

"Nah, how about we do a movie night instead, maybe even play a few childhood board games? Let's do something different, are you down?"

"Girl, I never would imagine Shellie Janae Moore would want to be at home on a Saturday night to play board games. Are you okay? Do you have a fever?"

"No, you said something that made me realize I do need to change if I want better and Girl, I do want better. Entering our 30's really opens up a new perspective! Going to bed at 29 immature and waking up 30 wanting to save the world, my soul, and lead someone to God. Do you think those thoughts, that premonition happens for everyone, or did God specify it for me?"

"I don't know Girl, I would say it happened for me as well, but I've always wanted to do good and be around good people. I think that's how you get ahead in life! Anyway, so Shellie, do you want to change for you or for Pastor Alonzo?"

"Ummm. . . So Trish, I honestly want to change for me. I have a great career and a wonderful life. I'm exfoliating, taking vitamins, and drinking water daily! So, I must be on to something. Pastor Alonzo would be an added bonus. One that I didn't think I needed or deserved."

Shellie, even though she appeared confident, had the worst self-esteem. One of those females you wonder, Girl is your mirror broken. But again, it's self-esteem and nobody can help you with a personal demon.

"Ho Ho Ho!! Happy Holidays!!"

Shellie kept her word and volunteered at the local shelter with Trish by her side. Alex tagged along and Pastor Alonzo noticing her. What could go wrong? I mean, all she had to do was scoop the food on a plate and cordially entertain. Seems simple, right? Shellie found a way to confront a few homeless individuals. They didn't form the line the correct way, so she provided reprimand.

They asked for extra, she stated, *"This isn't Burger King, you can't have it your way."*

Trish was quite different, she was overheard, *"I pray you have a wonderful day, stay warm be blessed."*

Why can't Shellie be more like Trish? I mean they've been together for years, shouldn't some of Trish's kindness rub off on Shellie.

Trish whispers in Shellie's ear, *"First Lady material remember."*

Her gait became a little more straight and her attitude diminished!

"Damn, I don't know what's wrong with me?"

Let's interlude there, Shellie grew up with loving parents. They devoted their time and effort to make sure her and her brother succeeded. However, Shellie always carried a "I must make them proud" mentality. To the point she only wanted to please them but never herself. Even when people provided praise for something good she did, there was always an underlying reason let her tell it. However, she's doing better. I mean I have to say that right, I am her best friend!! Well, I don't mind calling her out on her infractions, that's what makes real friendships!!

"Shellie, here comes the Pastor. . ."

"Really? How does my makeup look, am I cute?"

"Yes Girl, you look good. Now, turn around."

"Sis. Shellie, it's great to see you giving back to your community. Hello, Trish and. . ."

"Hello Pastor, this is my friend Alex."

The two shook hands, "It's nice to meet you."

"You as well."

He peered back to Shellie; her elegant glow and beautiful smile captivated his attention; he didn't want to make a scene. In due time, in due time!

"I will see you all at church tomorrow. And Shellie, maybe you'll be on time. I'm speaking it in the atmosphere now Sis. Shellie!!"

"I'm touching and agreeing with you Pastor," Shellie reached over and grazed Pastor's hand. He didn't back away; honestly, he didn't want her to move.

Shellie found a decent parking spot. She was two minutes early for worship! Trish was already in the pews; Miss always does right believes if you are 15 minutes early, you're right on time. Ha! Ha! That philosophy doesn't even apply at work. But oh well!

"Look at Pastor greeting the Saints with his beautiful smile and firm handshake! Okay Lord, a First Lady is always cordial. And I'm ready to enter his courts with praise!! Here we go."

"Pastor Alonzo and Deacon Tim it's so good to see you two this morning."

"Truly, today is an amazing day in which God saw fit for us to see. Sis. Shellie, it's even better since you've graced us with your presence and look a minute early."

"Now wait Pastor, I was two minutes early. I had to do some adjusting in the car but give me my credit."

They both laughed, Deacon Tim less than amused said, "Welcome."

Shellie entered the church Trish almost fainted and she even sat towards the opposite end of the pew so I wouldn't have to walk over anyone!

"Today will be great, thank the Lord, I can feel it!! Announcements are as follows; Pastor Alonzo would like to thank every member that showed up to help serve food to the homeless. Today is the final day for Toys for Tots, we still need a few more gifts to complete our yearly donation of 200. Please get those to me or Pastor by 3:00 today!"

Trish whispered, "Shellie did you bring the toys!"

"Yep, I sure did. I'll get them and bring them in after service!"

Trish wasn't sure if it was her prayers, Pastors motivation, or simply Shellie wanting to do right! But she was so proud of her friend!

"Oh, one last announcement, this year for Watch Night service we are asking volunteers to bring pastries to complete the catered breakfast. And that's all, have a blessed week Saints!!"

"Service was so good today. I'm so glad God is a forgiving and merciful God, I asked Him to forgive my attitude towards the homeless. And for the seen and unseen actions that I possess. Lord knows, my name has to be in the Lamb Book of Life, even if it's on the last page."

"Shellie, it takes more than a weekend."

"I know Girl, I know! Well, let me go get the gifts and bring them in. I'll be back."

Shellie's personality today was unmatched. All the positivity to be better, do better, and want better was written on her face. She smiled, and actually was in church for the Reach Out and Touch section of the service.

"Sis. Brown, here are a few donations from Trish and I, I know the kids will love them!"

"Thank you Shelby."

Shellie, paused for a moment, then stated, "Oh it's Shellie."

"Oh. . . Okay. Whatever!!"

"Listen here Sis. Brown, I can take my gifts. . ." Her thoughts were blocked by Pastors succulent voice.

"Sis. Shellie, thank you for the gifts. I'm sure the kids will enjoy them!"

Shellie thought, *"OOOOH, Sis. Brown better be glad Pastor saved her from my wrath!!"* She continued okay, *"Lord listen please. . . If I'm trying to do right, why do these heathens try me!!!"*

"Sis. Shellie, I wanted to ask you something. However, I don't want you to feel pressured to answer." Shellie's hands were clammy, she wanted to scream, Yesss! But she waited.

"I've been praying on this and I wanted to know. . . will you be the leader of the Toys for Tots?"

"Yessss, Yesss I'll, huh. . . wait, will I what?"

"Be the leader of the Toys for Tots??"

"Oh. . . that. . . Yes, I don't mind."

"Okay great, can you meet me here at 5:30, we will separate the toys and send them to their respective places."

"Of course Pastor, see you then!!"

"I think she was expecting a different question. Either way, I'll be able to talk to her later when she arrives."

Pastor had it all planed, it would just be Sis. Shellie and himself. Something like a date but keeping it very professional as well. Get to know the real her while doing God's work!

Ring Ring!! "Trish you left too soon, Pastor asked me to meet him back at the church this evening and lead the Toys for Tots for the church."

"What did you say?"

"Well, I thought he was about to ask me out so I uttered Yessss in a very ratchet voice."

"Oh Lord! Then what?"

"He was receptive and said he would see me then. So, what should I wear?"

"Umm!! Shellie, it isn't a date. BUT, make him lose consciousness in the most Godly divine way! Don't you have a shirt with a scripture on it or something?"

"Yes."

"Okay wear that and a pair of jeans."

"Bet!! Shellie, do you know all the "educated" words you were taught!"

"Umm, yes I do."

"Well, starting at 5:30 use those!" They both laughed.

Shellie had a tendency to be a little more ratchet than Trish. However, what fun would she be if her personality didn't shine through just a little.

Skuuuuurrrtttt!!! Shellie was driving like a crazy person, she arrived to the church parking lot at 5:27. With three minutes to spare, she checked her appearance in the mirror with pleasure. Pastor Alonzo exited his study. *Shellie should be here any minute now.* Shellie strutted into the church, meeting Pastor A in the foyer. The two locked eyes, then shyly looked away!

"Hello Sis. Shellie."

"Hello Pastor A!"

"Well, let's get started shall we?"

"Yes, let's!"

For what seemed like a lifetime, Shellie and Pastor A combed through the gifts with attempts to separate boys and girls toys, bikes, and small devices. They discussed their lives, childhood, college, favorite color, favorite ice cream. When done, Pastor A was more than impressed and Shellie; speechless!

Her thoughts, *"I can't wait to tell Trish."*

The pair discussed future plans for dinner and a movie. Shellie wanted to make a good first impression, she spoke well as Trish instructed but allowed her personality to show at times. They laughed; Shellie laughed so hard she cried!

"A man, a Godly man, who knows God, who isn't afraid to be vulnerable in conversation. But most importantly, makes me laugh to the point of gasping for air! "Yessss Lord!!! I've always heard, opposites attract. I've also heard rip up Your list!!"

"Thank you Pastor Michael Todd!! Now, it's time for intentional dating. Let's see where the road leads us." The two parted with a gentle embrace!!

Walking to the car Shellie thought, *"Lord, he smells good, Dolce and Gabbana light-blue, I know that fragrance anywhere."*

She grabbed her phone, smiling from ear to ear, she had to make one phone call.

"Heyyy Trish!! Girrlll, it was perfect, absolutely perfect! He was so gentle with my feelings, he made me laugh so hard I had tears streaming down my face! We are going out again next week."

"I'm so happy for you Shellie. See, Tyrone was simply a distraction! What God had for you was right under your nose, you just didn't see it!!"

"Trish I know. Girl I know! Pastor Alonzo discussed purpose with me, we discussed dating with intention! On the first interaction. Now, I know for a fact, I haven't discussed intentional dating with anyone."

"Well Shellie, here's your start!"

These past few months have been amazing! Pastor Alonzo is simply the most loving man I've ever met. We've been on countless dates, I'm always in anticipation of the next! He sends me flowers unexpectedly. Leaves little notes for me to apprehend. I mean God, You were truly looking out for me!

Alex and Trish are also doing well! I don't think she's ever been this happy!! She deserves it and more. We've double dated, Trish and I chant "Boaz is that you" from time to time, the men simply say "Yes."

Life is amazing right now! If someone told me, I would be dating Pastor A, celibate, and happy! I would've laughed the most gut wrenching laugh! But here I am killing it! Loving every moment and embracing what's to come!

Over these months the most important thing learned "try something different" step out of your comfort zone, go get everything you are destined to have! Go be everything you are destined to be! Do so with friends, family, and love. But most importantly, do so with God!! Oh and for those curious Saints, I paid my tithes this month, have you?

The End

STORY III

Desiree's Desire

"Live Right!! Holy and acceptable unto Christ!!!"

Ohhhh chilllee, they never cease to amaze me, trying to be holier than thou Christians as if the stone didn't hit them a time or two. Out here chanting and protesting for what?!! Listen, don't get me wrong, God is amazing, but some of His children get on my last nerve!! The hypocritical ones, those who judge, the noncommitting ones, back stabbers, you know those. Those same individuals who portray something different in the church yet hold a different position in the streets. Just be real, we are all imperfect people searching for something. Growing up in the church is one thing, but you have to be more committed to your own growth and development when your parents aren't forcing you six days out of a week.

I'm one of His children too, but I'm also an escort, I make my living by performing at maximum capacity for men that can't seem to reach their peak performance with their significant others. Do I like my job? Hell no? I'd rather be home playing Chutes and Ladders with my kid. But, here I am waiting on John number 7 for the night! My husband, yes that's right, I have a husband. He supports me, basically he met me this way. Besides, we have our plan thought out and it requires a lot of financial responsibility. Before you go judging me and my lifestyle take a look into your life, you out here sexing men for free, at least they pay me!! Right?!?!

Let me introduce myself, I'm Desire by night and Desiree by day. I'm a 25-year-old escort, I've been escorting since I was 16. My mom kicked me out when I was pregnant with Desmond. She told me, the only legs that should be open in her house, was her legs! The only way to make it was to turn a few tricks. See, when I say Christians try to be holier than thou, I need y'all to understand, some of my most faithful clients are from the church. You may refer to them as Brother so and so. I just say John number whatever I'm on for the night. Honey they pay well, they tip well, so there's no bashing them personally. Besides, what good would that do for all the things I have listed on my vision board. The way I see it, I'll be done with all of this before I'm 27. Every John gives me roughly $1,000; depending on what services they want. Most nights, I leave making $7,000 and some of y'all don't make that in a month!! Anyway, my husband, told me, we got to run up a check, but also be safe doing it.

"Desmond, come get dressed, your Daddy will be here any minute to pick you up."

"Mama, do I have to go with him again this week! All we do is talk about boring sh. . ."

"Boy if you don't watch your mouth!!"

"Okay Mama, I mean all we do is talk about the weather."

"Being a storm chaser can't be that enjoyable."

"I'm 9 years old almost 10, I like all kinds of sports. If it weren't for Trey, I don't know what I would do! Mama, are you listening to me?!"

"Yes Child, now go get dressed before he pulls up and you know talking to him more than I have to gives me a headache. Remember, he is your father, one night the rubber broke and that's all she wrote!! But I love you as if you were planned."

"Now Mama, you had no business with no man half a hundred when you were a teenager."

"Desmond, I told you I wouldn't lie to you, so don't make me relive that craziness. I love you; he loves you, and that's all that matters, now hurry up!"

"Ha! Ha! Des, I don't know why you make that boy go with that old man."

"Trey, that's his father. Whether we want him to be or not. I met you a few years later, even though you didn't look at me like that doesn't mean other men didn't. You already know the story of how Desmond got here, I didn't have a choice. His father sends his little funky $400 a month, so the least we can do is send him when he asks."

"Okay Des, whatever you say."

"Desmond, Desmond, your Daddy is here."

(Doorbell Ding)

My previous John turned baby's father. Larry is the name. We're at a good place now. Being mad at him didn't do any good. Not working for months caused my frustrations to get the best of me. However, Larry provided for what we needed. He was a great man. The circumstances which lead us together for the rest of our natural lives, well, that's a different story. This man couldn't get anything right, one night when I was 15, we met at a hotel, he wanted the platinum package which included the "works" and an overnight stay. 9 months later, Desmond was here. Luckily, I knew exactly who he belonged to. In my best Maury voice, "Larry you are the father!!" Larry's a good father, he is boring, but I mean he's old enough to be Desmond papa. No other children, never married, so Desmond is his life. Don't get me wrong, Trey is an absolutely amazing father. But when it comes to stability Larry is more seasoned hands down!

"Hey, Larry, what are y'all doing this weekend?"

"Hey, DD, probably catch a movie, chase a storm if one comes rolling in, do some yard work, and take my little man to the mall. Nothing too serious, I just want to spend as much time with him as possible."

"You don't have to tell me your plans DD, one day you'll stop."

"Yeah. Eventually I will."

"Anyway, Desmond, enjoy time with your dad, be on your best behavior. I love you and I'll see you soon."

Grunting, "I love you too Mama."

It's Friday, my phone is blowing up with Johns, it's time to get to work.

"Trey, I'm leaving, I'll see you at some point

tonight or tomorrow."

Money talks, and as always, be safe, love you Desiree."

Before judgement arises, let me introduce myself. The name is Trey, I'm married to the beautiful Desiree or Desire depending on how you know her. Some would say I'm crazy, who would actually marry an escort.

Let me explain, several years ago, Desiree and Desmond were at a restaurant, "The Waffle House" and it was late. Extremely late. Wondering why they could be there, I asked if everything was okay? Desiree with the slightest attitude said, "we're fine." For some reason, Desmond made eye contact with me like never before, with desperation in his eyes. I knew something needed to be done.

After some hesitation, Desiree and I exchanged numbers. We discussed the infamous first date questions, what's your favorite this and that. She finally confessed to her lifestyle of choice. I fell in love with her mind, her beauty, and her ability to adapt to any situation. Her being an escort didn't decipher my choice, it actually brought us closer. See, I'm a man, a Black man at that. My nature is to protect, provide, establish security, and all that. What Desiree needed was a man by her side as she weathered the storm, non-judgmental. We've all fallen short of Gods glory, and believe me, He's not going to ask you about my sins nor about Desiree's once we get to those Pearly Gates. Nonetheless, I fell in love with Desiree, Desire is a name given to her alter ego. Ensuring her safety is my main concern, we share each other's location indefinitely. Yes, even though I trust her, I know she's making a living. There's no trust for the men she attracts. However, I can't change her path, I can only enhance her future. That's what my intentions are pure and without regret.

I love both Desiree and Desmond, nobody can

change that! So leave the judging to Jesus!!

Alright! John number 2 is in route and I'm done for the night. Trey is just getting off work and there's something special I want to do for him tonight. We don't get to spend a lot of time together, but tonight it's all about us. Matter of fact, I took off the rest of the weekend.

Desmond is with his dad which means kid free!!! We won't be chasing any storms, but I'm sure we will be chasing shots with lime.

(Ring Ring)

"Hey, Baby is everything okay?"

"Yes Trey, everything is good."

"Can you run me a hot bath, throw in some of those bath salts I like, and unlock the door?"

"Yes, what's going on, it's not even 7:00, you're already done?"

"Yes, okay, well it's unlocked, I'll have your items in the bathroom waiting on you. Candles or nah?”

"Oh yes, Baby candles!”

Trey was excited, see, he tries to play the role of supportive husband. But in all honesty, he couldn't wait for Desiree to come home, safe, and actually quit doing what she's doing. Desmond is getting older, he's starting to pick up on little cues, and she doesn't lie to him. It's only a matter of time before he realizes his mother is an escort. Luckily, the upkeep of our community and her hours of operation make things unnoticeable. She wears scrubs when she leaves the house and when she returns, so nobody asks. Oh, and she drives nearly an hour for work!

"Welcome home! I would ask how everything went but it's that grey area that bothers me each time I ask. So, I'm glad you're home. All the necessity items are in the bathroom and I'll see you for kisses and loving when you get out.”

Desiree took countless showers daily, secretly,

she wanted to discontinue what she was doing, but the money is so good and the lifestyle is even better! We drive foreign, take trips, and buy stock. But, we're saving for a beautiful 1.5 million dollar beach front house where the neighbors are roughly three miles apart. Just a little while longer and we'll get it.

"So Baby, I got off early, I just wanted to spend some time with my man! I know that doesn't come around too often. Let's make the best of it. What should we do first?"

"After your bath, how about we get dressed and head Downtown. I'm sure Downtown L.A. has a lot to offer us on a Friday! Starting with some grub, I'm hungry."

"I was just about to find something to eat and watch a game when you called me Desi."

"Okay, well I'll be out in a little while and we can go out. Stay out all night if we want, maybe get a room Downtown and come back Sunday."

"Wait. Desi you don't have to work tomorrow?"

"No more work tonight either?"

"No Baby, I'm yours all weekend."

"Well, in that case, yes, let's pack a bag and spend the weekend in Downtown L.A., there's plenty for us to do."

Going Downtown was a potential risk, running into one of Desire's Johns. But luckily, that hasn't happened yet. Furthermore, she's going to change, she's got so much to live for, to be present for. I just have to show her everything she needs is home.

"I'm so happy to be home early, I can't wait to be in Trey's arms all weekend. Hit up a few bars, beaches, and relaxation. This will be great!"

"Okay Trey, I'm done. What did you pack?"

"Just some beach clothes, a few shirts, shorts, and that's about it. Should I bring some fancier clothes?"

"Nah Babe, I honestly want to keep it casual. Nothing too serious, just quality time. Can you handle that?"

"Oh, no doubt Desi, I can handle that."

"It's a beautiful night Babe."

Desiree and Trey booked a room Downtown; they sat out on the balcony overlooking spectators and beach goers. It was an absolute perfect night. They enjoyed a few laughs, people watching, and cold glasses of wine.

Feeling good, Desiree stated, "Trey I'm done!"

"Done? Done with what?"

"Escorting. I don't want you to be upset with me because I know the money is good. But, I can't do it anymore. It makes me feel dirty now. I mean yes, at the beginning I did it to provide for Desmond. However, now I'm tired. I just want you to have my body, nobody else. I know you are supportive of whatever I decide, so can you support me in this?"

"Hell yes Desi."

And with tears streaming down her face, she whispered, "Really?"

"Listen, when I met you, I fell in love with your heart, it was a lot to handle concerning the escorting business. However, if I wanted to be with you and Desmond, I had to accept all of you. So I did!! I didn't like it at first, I mean, I actually don't like it now to be honest. But, it was your way of thinking. You had to find your own way, I accepted that and stood beside you. However, what man in his right mind would want his lady to be intimate with someone else? I know the love and connection isn't there, you are doing a "job" but still you're mine. We vowed to love each other for better or worse. I meant those vows Baby! I swear I did! I love you Desiree, I can't stand when you have to be Desire."

"So what now? What type of job are you interested in? Or being a stay at home mom would suffice?"

"Honestly, baking gives me such great peace. You always tell me my pie, cookies, and cakes should be in a bakery. Maybe starting a business would be ideal. What do you think?"

"The sky is honestly the limit, you are tenacious,

driven, competitive, the market could use someone like you. Go for it!! Be someone you are proud of. You know when you mentioned quitting just now, you developed a twinkle in your eye. I'm not sure if I even seen that side of you before."

"Trey, before escorting, my vision wasn't clear. Honestly, my mother always ridiculed me for being promiscuous. Because of her words, the world of escorting became a reality. I was good at it. But what she failed to understand she woke a beast. Yes, 16 and pregnant. I touched more money than most dream of. There were nights Desmond woke up in a different hotel than what he went to sleep in. However, going back to a place where my mother said I wasn't going to make it or I wasn't good enough for this or that. Kept me driven! So now, at 25, I'm ready for new beginnings. I don't have to prove to her I can do it because I made it out. I'm grateful for you Trey, you were able to see passed my escorting to see my heart. For that I'm grateful.

Thank you for being patient with me, loving me, and loving Desmond. That wasn't an easy task but you stepped in and led us. So, I'm doing this for us. Today was my last day!! Desire is dead! Desiree is alive and she's ready to bake!! I love you Boy."

"I love you too, Girl!!"

"Welcome home Desmond! How was your weekend?"

"Hey Mom, let's just say I'm so glad to be home. What did y'all do without me?"

"Come in here, let's sit down and talk!!"

"Oh Nooo, am I in trouble?"

"No Baby, it's all good news. Desmond we, well, I wanted to discuss something with you. We've been conversing for a while about moving and starting over on a beach front house. You were excited, just as you are now. What if we said, were going to stay here? I'm going to open up a small bakery and live out my dream. What are your thoughts?

"Well, Mom, Dad, I really love the beach, the water seemed so nice. But, if this is what's best for us, then let's stay here. Besides, who likes packing boxes anyway. So, what about your other job Mom?"

"Huh? What? Oh, I'm going to quit. Actually, I resigned this weekend."

"And the Johns?"

"Wait a minute, what do you mean Johns?"

"Mom, I'm almost 10, I'm no fool. You leave all times of the night, your phone rings all times of the day. You are dressed like a "nurse" in scrubs, but I know for a fact, you don't have a nursing license. Besides, I went through your phone one day. I mean what did you expect?"

Trey and Desiree looking confused and baffled, stated together, "Well, umm, do you have any questions?"

"No, I looked up "Johns" on the internet and after

I added a description. I pretty much know what you do. It's disgusting, how could you even do that? Don't say it's for me, don't say it's for money because that's the least of our worries. So, that's how you met my dad isn't it? Wow!! This is horrible! I'm so glad nobody knows because I would be the talk of the lunchroom! I'm glad you're quitting, I've been holding this in for months, yuck!!"

Trey interjected, "Desmond, Desmond, don't do your mom like that!"

"And you, how can you even let her do that? Can I be excused?? PLEASE!!!"

Desiree with tears in her eyes and gasping for air, exited the room to the back patio.

"I'm so sorry, I'm so sorry!! God, You know my heart. I promise I did this for us! But I'm done. I can't hurt anyone else."

"Good morning Desmond."

"Good morning Mom. Mom, I'm sorry about last night, but getting that off my chest needed to be done. I just love you Mom and if what I read was true. It was all too much to handle!!"

"What did you read Desmond?"

"The title was escort; you have sex with multiple men in a night and they pay you money. But some people were even killed or hurt by their Johns. Is that true?"

"Yes Baby, that's true. However, nothing has happened to me and I'm thankful to God for it. I'm done, I promise Baby, I'm done."

"Okay Mom, okay. So, what are we doing today?"

"Since, I don't have any plans nor I don't have work; maybe we can go to the mall and have a mother/son date. Would you like that?"

"Yes, we haven't did that in a while."

"Well, after breakfast, let's get dressed and head out. Trey is at work until this evening. Is that fine?"

"Yes Mom, that's cool."

"Desmond, I don't remember the last time we actually spent time together during the workday."

"Mom. . . That's because we haven't. I knew your job was demanding; I'm glad it's over now, though. So, what's next for Desiree? When should we expect the bakery?"

"Really soon Baby. I know there's a lot that comes with the bakery, but the plans to move forward are definitely in the works. Desmond, do you have any questions about my previous line of work?"

"Not really Mom. Do you know Siri knows everything! I mean, I asked, I got more than what I thought, but she told me so much!! I wish you wouldn't have kept a secret from me though."

"How about we make a pact."

"What's that?"

"Ask Siri."

"Yo, Siri. . ."

"I'm kidding Boy, it's like making a deal, confirming a secret.

"Oh ok, well yes, let's make a pact."

"I promise I am done being an escort. Being home with you every night is far more rewarding, besides Trey and you bring so much love and joy to my life. I'm ditching desire and found my way to Desiree!!"

The End

ABOUT THE AUTHOR

My name is Rayven Manigo, I'm a small town girl with big dreams. This is my second book, one which I embraced a different realm of writing. The second time around, I still sit, a mother, a daughter, a sister, a friend, and now an author.

I enjoy worshipping God, family time, traveling, reading, and spending as much time as possible with my heart in human form.

In these stories you will find all walks of life, some of my own, some of others, but most importantly I hope you feel each one and relate to the message.

Thank you for taking the time to read, may God bless you richly!